Dear Parents and Teachers,

Reading chapter books is a very exciting step in your child's life as a reader.

With Hello Reader Chapter Books, our goal is to bring the excitement of chapter books together with appropriate content and vocabulary so that children take pride in their success as readers.

Children like to read independently, but you can share this experience with them to make it even more rewarding. Here are some tips to try:

- *Read the book aloud for the first time.*
- *Point out the chapter headings.*
- *Look at the illustrations. Can your child find words in the text that match the pictures?*
- *After you or your child finishes reading a chapter, ask what might happen in the next chapter.*
- *Praise your child throughout the reading of the book.*
- *And if your child wants to read alone, then take out your own book or magazine and read sitting side by side!*

Remember, reading is a joy to share. So, have fun experiencing your child's new ability to read chapter books!

Francie Alexander
Vice President and Chief Academic Officer
Scholastic Education

To Jeff and Michelle
—G.M.

For my Dad, who never left my side while working on this book
and who will always be in my heart. I miss you.
Love, Tam

ISBN 0-439-66434-9

Text copyright © 2004 by Grace Maccarone.
Illustrations copyright © 2004 by Tammie Lyon.
All rights reserved. Published by Scholastic Inc.

12 11 10 9 8 7 6 5 4 3 2 1   9 10 11 12/0

Printed in the U.S.A.
First printing, May 2004

IT'S GRADUATION DAY!

by Grace Maccarone
Illustrated by Tammie Lyon

SCHOLASTIC INC.

New York   Toronto   London   Auckland   Sydney
Mexico City   New Delhi   Hong Kong   Buenos Aires

CHAPTER 1

Matt is getting dressed.
He has a gown and a hat.

The hat is flat on top.
It's a graduation cap!

"I want it," says Pat.
"No," says Matt.
"This hat is for me."

"This year, I learned to read and write.
That means I will graduate today."

"Can I graduate, too?" Pat asks.
"Not yet," Matt answers.

Pat is sad.

"Can I have a hat?" Pat asks.

Matt finds a hat.
Pat is happy.

Matt, Pat, and Mom walk to school.

CHAPTER 2

Oops!
Matt's hat falls off.
He puts it back on.

Matt's hat falls off again!
Matt puts it on again.

He keeps his head very, very still.
He walks very, very slowly.

Matt sees Jane.
Jane is in his class.

Jane runs and jumps and spins.

Matt stays very still.
"Why are you standing like that?"
Jane asks.
"I don't want my hat to fall off again,"
Matt says.

"My hat doesn't fall off,
even when I do this!"
Jane does a cartwheel.
Her hat stays on her head.

"How does your hat stay on?"
Matt asks.
"Did you use glue?"

Jane laughs.
"No! I used hairpins!"

Jane gives a few hairpins to Matt.

CHAPTER 3

In the gym, everyone waits for graduation to begin.

The children sit in the front rows.
Everyone is excited.

The principal calls the name
of every boy and girl.

Matt waits for his name.
Then it will be his turn to graduate.

Matt hears the principal call his name

"Happy graduation!" says the principal.

Matt is happy.
His mom is proud.
Graduation is over.
Mom gives Matt a kiss.

Pat hops over to Matt.
She gives him a kiss, too.

"We will get pizza for lunch," Mom say

"Yay!" Matt shouts.

Matt throws his hat in the air.
Pat throws her hat in the air, too.

It's a happy graduation!